STAR WARS™

FACE OFF

29 WILD AND WACKY MATCHUPS!

WRITTEN BY
ARIE KAPLAN

ILLUSTRATED BY
DAVID WHITE

FOR AVIYA LEAH KAPLAN.
THE FORCE IS STRONG IN THIS ONE.

ISBN 978-0-545-92541-9

10 9 8 7 6 5 4 3 2 1 16 17 18 19 20

PRINTED IN THE U.S.A. 40

FIRST PRINTING 2016

BOOK DESIGN BY ERIN MCMAHON

HEY, GUESS WHAT, YOU LUCKY READER?

In the following pages, you'll see the LEGO *Star Wars* characters duke it out against one another. These are the coolest matchups ever in the history of cool matchups that are matched up in a manner that is cool! (Impressed? You SHOULD be.) For each battle, you'll get all the stats and info you need to decide who you think might win. The last page features the experts' rulings on each duel. Who ARE these experts? How should WE know? If we knew, we'd be the experts!

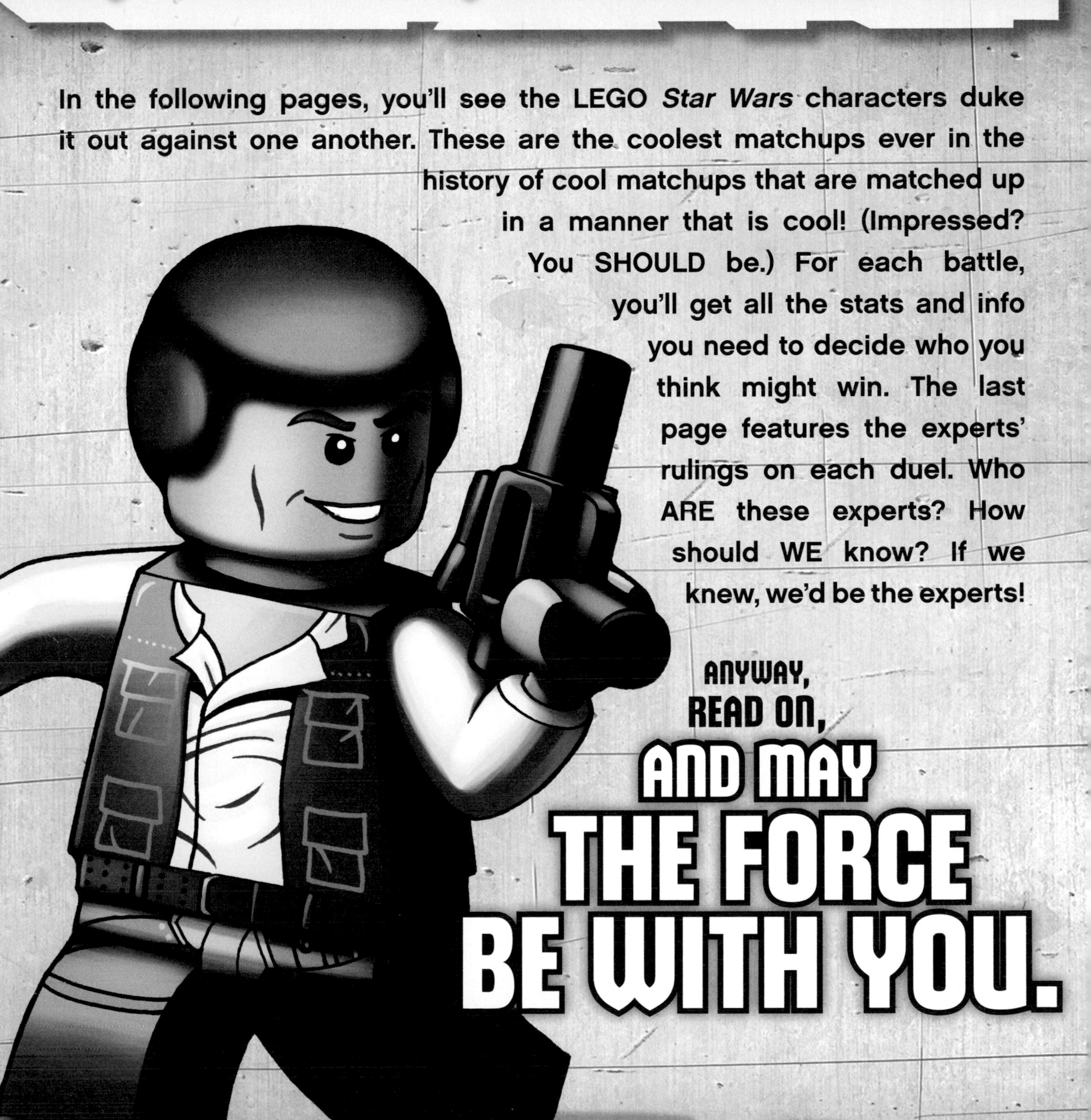

ANYWAY, READ ON, AND MAY THE FORCE BE WITH YOU.

CHEWBACCA VS. JAWAS

Chewbacca is a hulking giant with too much body hair—basically a cross between a werewolf and a basketball player. The Jawas are . . . not. They're each about as tall as a "fun size" candy bar. What if the Jawas and Chewbacca were locked in combat? Well, there's three of THEM and only one of HIM, so . . . there's THAT.

HOMEWORLD: KASHYYYK, THE PLANET OF GIANT, FURRY, FANGED MONSTERS WHO ARE, IRONICALLY, SUPER NICE

AFFILIATION: COPILOT, REBEL ALLIANCE; PRESIDENT, HAIR CLUB FOR WOOKIEES

SPECIES: WOOKIEE (SUBSPECIES: COPILOT)

WEAPONS: BOWCASTER; BANDOLIER STRAP; BAD BREATH

SPECIAL MOVE: "ARM-PULLER-OUTER" MANEUVER

STATS

INTELLIGENCE

STRENGTH

AGILITY

DAMAGE

CONTROL

COURAGE

SHAGGINESS

THE SHOWDOWN

You might think that the Wookiee would mop the floor with the Jawas, no question. NOT SO FAST! What if they're hiding WEAPONS inside those robes? If any one of these Jawas is smuggling a baby grand piano and decides to drop it on Chewbacca's head, the match is over before the Wookiee has time to say "RRROOOAAARR."

JAWAS

HOMEWORLD: TATOOINE, THE DESERT PLANET (BASICALLY A BEACH PLANET WITHOUT ALL THE PESKY WATER.)

AFFILIATION: HOARDERS ANONYMOUS

WEAPONS: ION BLASTER. WHATEVER THE JAWAS' WEAPONS ARE, YOU CAN GUARANTEE THEY'RE SECONDHAND, LIKE ALL THEIR OTHER JUNK.

SPECIAL MOVE: CAN GET THE MOST STYLISH HOODED ROBES FOR HALF OFF!

STATS

Stat	Rating
INTELLIGENCE	●●●●●
STRENGTH	●●●●●●
AGILITY	●●●●●●●
DAMAGE	●●●●
CONTROL	●●●●
COURAGE	●●
HOODIES	●●●●●●●●●

HOTH LUKE VS. TROPICAL DARTH MAUL

Jedi Knights like Luke Skywalker can adapt to ANY environment, even Hoth, which is like a big ol' refrigerator shaped like a planet. But Luke's skill at making perfect snow angels has done little to prepare him for the killer reflexes and tacky clothing of Tropical Darth Maul! Darth Maul may LOOK like a tattooed pineapple, but Luke shouldn't underestimate him!

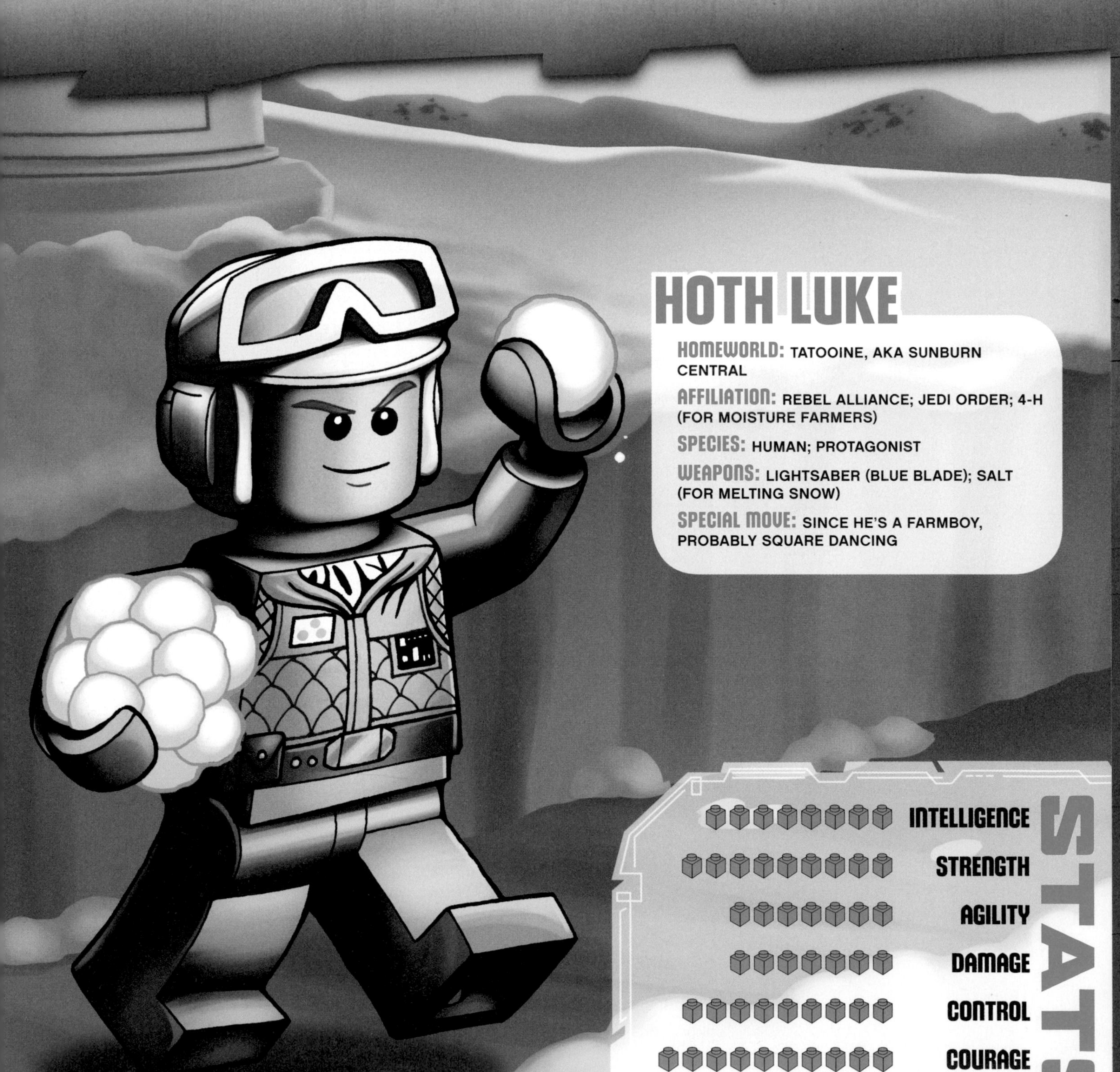

THE SHOWDOWN

Darth Maul has a double-bladed lightsaber, but Luke isn't scared. He can use the Force to hurl a volley of snowballs at Maul's laser-sword, short-circuiting the wicked weapon! When Hoth Luke's around, the weather outside IS frightful, so Tropical Darth Maul uses the tools at his disposal: mainly, mad limbo skills, sand ("it gets everywhere!"), and those horn-thingies on his head!

TROPICAL DARTH MAUL

HOMEWORLD: DATHOMIR (WELL, SUBURBAN DATHOMIR)

AFFILIATION: SITH ORDER; RED-LIGHTSABER-HAVERS CLUB

SPECIES: ZABRAK (AKA "THOSE GUYS WHO USE THEIR HORNS AS COAT HANGERS")

WEAPONS: DOUBLE-BLADED LIGHTSABER (RED BLADES); MENACING GLARE (RED EYES); TABASCO SAUCE (RED SAUCE)

SPECIAL MOVE: GETTING SLICED IN HALF LIKE A SANDWICH

STATS

Stat	Rating (bricks)
INTELLIGENCE	6
STRENGTH	10
AGILITY	4
DAMAGE	8
CONTROL	8
COURAGE	8
SWEET TATTOOS	10

QUI-GON JINN VS. COUNT DOOKU

You've heard of "Duel of the Fates"? This is "Duel of the Beards"! Dooku wants to make Qui-Gon "REAL GONE," but the veteran Jedi has a few tricks up his beard—er, sleeve! (And also probably in his beard.) Qui-Gon was Dooku's Padawan apprentice, but the two never got a chance to spar. What would happen if the pupil met the mustache—er, the master—in battle?

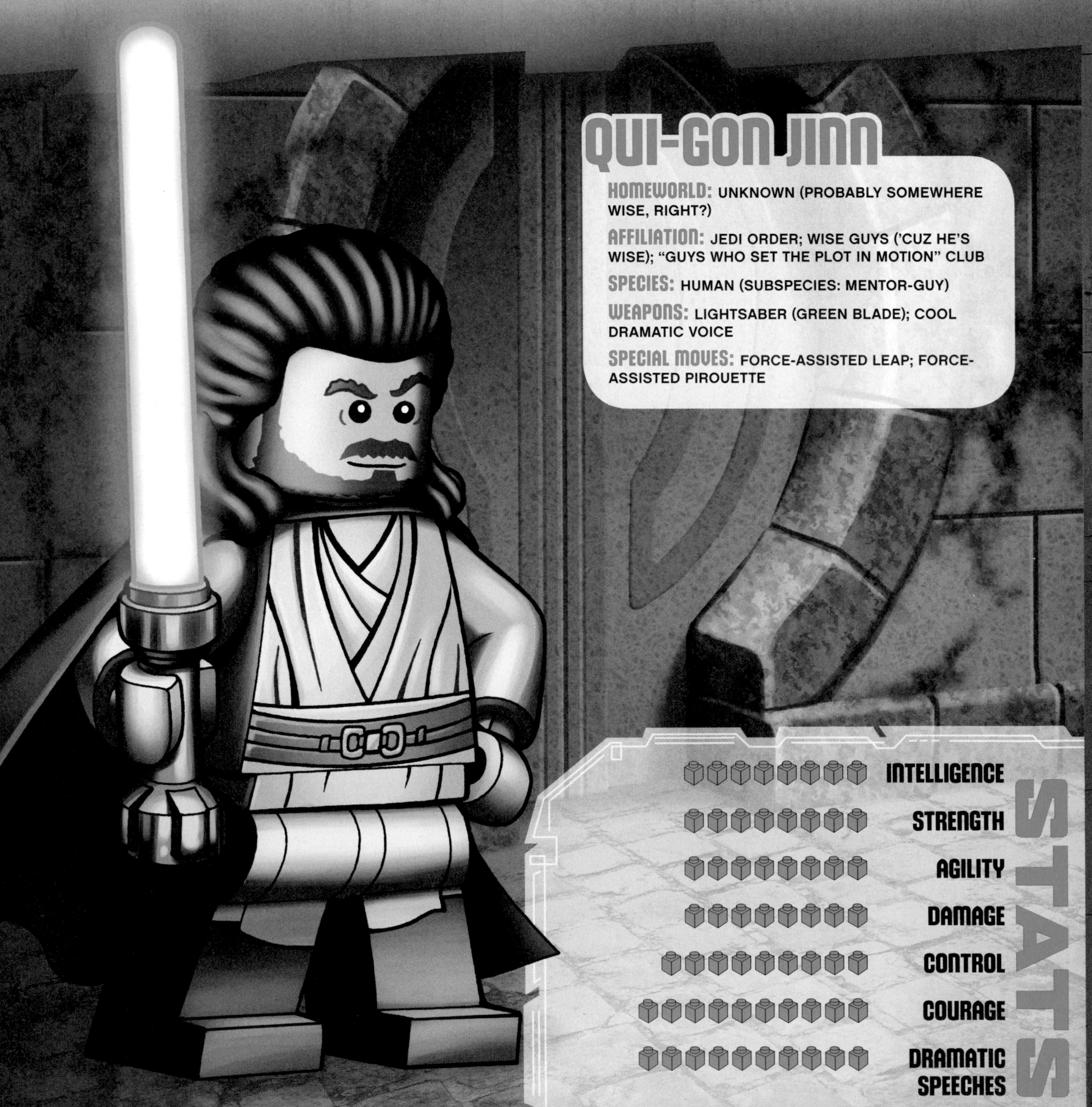

THE SHOWDOWN

Qui-Gon locks eyes with his former mentor, Count Dooku. Gone are the days when Dooku would tell Qui-Gon to sit up straight. Now Dooku would tell Qui-Gon to SITH up straight. Or something like that. As the two fearsome warriors move toward each other, an epic confrontation begins, with all the drama of something dramatic that has lots of drama. Drama!

HOMEWORLD: SERENNO (A PLANET WHERE BEING A COUNT IS STILL A THING!)

AFFILIATION: SITH ORDER; SEPARATIST ALLIANCE; VARIOUS OTHER EVIL GROUPS THAT START WITH *S*

SPECIES: HUMAN (SPECIFICALLY, EVIL HUMAN)

WEAPONS: LIGHTSABER (RED BLADE); JEWELRY ('CAUSE HE'S FANCY. HE IS A COUNT, Y'KNOW!)

SPECIAL MOVES: FORCE LIGHTNING; ABILITY TO GET HIS BUTT WHUPPED BY YODA

STATS

INTELLIGENCE

STRENGTH

AGILITY

DAMAGE

CONTROL

COURAGE

RESEMBLANCE TO MEAN OLD EAGLE

OBI-WAN KENOBI VS. THE INQUISITOR

One of the greatest Jedi versus one of the greatest Jedi-taker-outers! Many Jedi have fallen before the Inquisitor, the scariest guy to rock a turtleneck since . . . well, maybe EVER. The Inquisitor was trained BY Darth Vader, but Obi-Wan is the person who TRAINED VADER HIMSELF. In other words, the Inquisitor is really fighting the guy who trained the guy who trained HIM. Confused yet? WE sure are!

HOMEWORLD: STEWJON (BUT DOES HE EVER CALL OR WRITE? NO!)

AFFILIATION: JEDI KNIGHTS; ALSO, THE "DUDES WHO SOMETIMES WEAR ROBES" SOCIETY AND THE DESERT HERMITS GUILD (PROBABLY, RIGHT?)

SPECIES: HUMAN (BUT DON'T HOLD THAT AGAINST HIM)

WEAPONS: LIGHTSABER (COOL); THE FORCE (COOL); ARMORED WRIST GUARDS (NOT SO MUCH)

SPECIAL MOVE: SPIN ATTACK (WHICH WILL COME IN HANDY IF HE EVER FIGHTS A SPINNING TOP)

STATS

INTELLIGENCE

STRENGTH

AGILITY

DAMAGE

CONTROL

COURAGE

BEARD MAINTENANCE

THE SHOWDOWN

The Inquisitor mounts a potentially deadly surprise attack, lurking in the shadows. But Obi-Wan can sense his foe's presence. More than that, he can smell his foe, who reeks. The Inquisitor's lightsaber is double-bladed and he can even make the blades SPIN on the hilt. However, sometimes it's best to just use a lightsaber like a lightsaber (as Obi-Wan does) and not like a baton at band camp (like the Inquisitor). Oh, snap! It is on like Qui-Gon!

HOMEWORLD: UTAPAU, PLANET OF PEOPLE WITH YELLOW EYES AND YELLOWER TEETH

AFFILIATION: GALACTIC EMPIRE; INQUISITORS; LOYAL ORDER OF SCOWLY FACES (OKAY, THAT LAST ONE'S MADE UP)

SPECIES: PAU'AN, OR AS YOU MIGHT KNOW THEM, "THOSE LINEY-FACED GUYS WITH THE LINES ON THEIR FACES"

WEAPONS: LIGHTSABER (RED BLADE); SARCASM (WITHERING); FACE THAT WILL HAUNT YOUR NIGHTMARES (MOMMY!)

SPECIAL MOVE: LIGHTSABER SPINNING (SPINNAGE? SPINNERY? ANYWAY, HE CAN TWIRL IT REAL GOOD)

STATS

INTELLIGENCE	●●●●●●●●●
STRENGTH	●●●●●●●●●
AGILITY	●●●●●●●●
DAMAGE	●●●●●●
CONTROL	●●●●●●●●
COURAGE	●●●●●●●●●
BALDNESS	●●●●●●●●●●

LEIA VS. GREEDO

Princess Leia has tracked the Rodian outlaw Greedo to Tatooine, home of Luke Skywalker. Leia's intel tells her that Greedo means to harm Luke, who's back home making sure all his mail is getting forwarded to his new address. Is Leia gonna just sit idly by and watch her brother get picked off by something that looks like a green lemon with eyes?

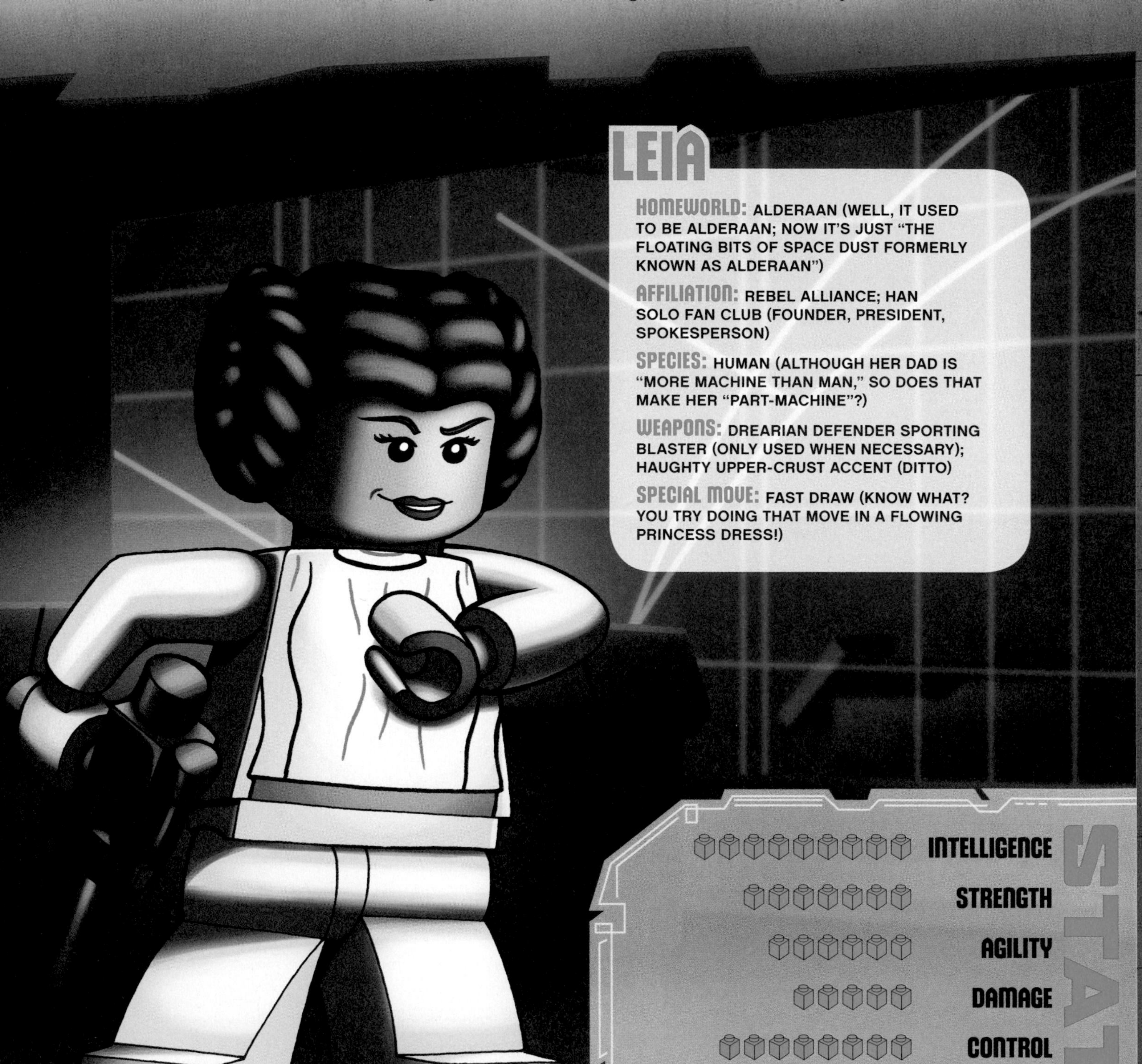

THE SHOWDOWN

Greedo shoots first and, as usual, he misses by a mile. Leia draws her weapon, and fires a warning shot near Greedo's head. Because it's a thick head, Greedo takes this as a challenge, and he charges forward. Leia won't give up, but neither will her dull-witted adversary. It's the Royal vs. the Rodian! Organa vs. the Outlaw! The Princess vs. the, um . . . Prickly-Headed Guy.

HOMEWORLD: TATOOINE, WHERE THE WEATHER REPORT IS ALWAYS "SUNNY AND DRY"

AFFILIATION: BOUNTY HUNTER (WELL, MAYBE SOMEDAY)

SPECIES: RODIAN (FOLKS WHO ARE AWFUL AT PLAYING "GOT YOUR NOSE" BECAUSE THEY, UM . . . DON'T HAVE NOSES)

WEAPON: LL-30 BLASTER PISTOL, FOR ALL YOUR BLASTING NEEDS

SPECIAL MOVE: QUICK DRAW (WELL, MAYBE SOMEDAY)

STATS

INTELLIGENCE

STRENGTH

AGILITY

DAMAGE

CONTROL

COURAGE

USELESSNESS

HAN SOLO VS. JANGO FETT

Once upon a time, Boba Fett had Han Solo frozen in carbonite like one of those "hard chocolate shell" ice cream bars. But what if Solo faced off against Boba Fett's father, Jango Fett? Who would win, the crafty Corellian smuggler, or the only bounty hunter alive whose name rhymes with mango?

HOMEWORLD: CORELLIA (HOME TO PIRATES AND SMUGGLERS)

AFFILIATION: REBEL ALLIANCE; VEST WEARERS' GUILD; GUYS WHOSE NAMES RHYME WITH YOLO

SPECIES: HUMAN (SUBSPECIES: SCOUNDREL)

WEAPON: MODIFIED BLASTER PISTOL (MODIFIED TO MAKE IT COOLER, LIKE ITS OWNER)

SPECIAL MOVE: TELLING CHEWIE TO "PUNCH IT!"

STATS

Stat	Bricks
INTELLIGENCE	6
STRENGTH	7
AGILITY	8
DAMAGE	6
CONTROL	8
COURAGE	10
ROGUISH CHARM	10

THE SHOWDOWN

Both opponents are roughly similar in size and build, but Jango Fett can always zoom away from trouble on his jetpack. And the masked bounty hunter has enough tricks up his heavily armored sleeve to easily win this match. But then again, Han Solo has a Wookiee for a best friend. So . . . there's that.

ANAKIN SKYWALKER VS. JEK-14

It's the battle of the millennium! A young guy with anger issues and Force powers vs. another young guy with anger issues and Force powers. They both know their way around a lightsaber, and they can both move things with their mind. But only Anakin has a sweet black tunic! Does that give him the advantage?

HOMEWORLD: TATOOINE (SPECIFICALLY, THE SANDY PART)

AFFILIATION: JEDI ORDER; "PALPATINE FOR EMPEROR" POLITICAL CAMPAIGN

SPECIES: HUMAN (EVENTUALLY, CYBORG—SPOILER ALERT!)

WEAPON: LIGHTSABER (BLUE BLADE, BUT EVENTUALLY RED—SPOILER ALERT!)

SPECIAL MOVE: ALWAYS HAVING SWEET HAIR

STATS

INTELLIGENCE

STRENGTH

AGILITY

DAMAGE

CONTROL

COURAGE

BROODING

THE SHOWDOWN

JEK-14 was cooked up like an evil dessert by Count Dooku and his evil cronies. On Dooku's orders, JEK-14 lashes out at Anakin with all the fury of an oncoming storm . . . a storm with one blue arm, for some reason. But he who underestimates a Skywalker courts (at the very least) a bad knee injury.

HOMEWORLD: KAMINO (SPECIFICALLY, COUNT DOOKU'S SUPER-SECRET, TOTALLY HUSH-HUSH CLONE MINI-LAB)

AFFILIATION: SITH ORDER; PCTDDDW (PEOPLE CREATED TO DO DOOKU'S DIRTY WORK)

SPECIES: WELL, HE'S A CLONE OF JANGO FETT CREATED BY COUNT DOOKU BY CHANNELING FORCE ENERGY INTO HIS CLONE CHAMBER VIA A KYBER CRYSTAL, SO . . . NONE?

WEAPONS: SCARY BLUE LIGHTSABER; SCARY BLUE ARM; SCARY BLUE EYES

SPECIAL MOVE: FORCE LIGHTNING (NOT FORCE THUNDER, FORCE RAIN, OR FORCE SUNSHINE)

STATS

INTELLIGENCE

STRENGTH

AGILITY

DAMAGE

CONTROL

COURAGE

SCARY BLUENESS

EZRA BRIDGER VS. BOBA FETT

Ezra Bridger is a teenager who's training to be a Jedi. He's basically a Jedi intern. That makes him a prime target for Boba Fett, who's an enemy of all Jedi . . . even the interns. It's the Semi-Jedi vs. the Lone Clone!

EZRA BRIDGER

HOMEWORLD: THE LOTHAL PLANET WHERE THE EMPIRE IS A SUPER-UNWELCOME HOUSEGUEST

AFFILIATION: REBEL NETWORK OF REALLY REBELLY REBELS

SPECIES: HUMAN (SUBSPECIES: MOPEY TEEN)

WEAPONS: LIGHTSABER/BLASTER COMBO, WHICH IS SO COOL IT ALMOST MAKES UP FOR THE "MOPEY TEEN" STUFF

SPECIAL MOVE: JEDI PUSH (HE'S A REALLY PUSHY KID)

STATS

- INTELLIGENCE
- STRENGTH
- AGILITY
- DAMAGE
- CONTROL
- COURAGE
- PICKPOCKETRY

THE SHOWDOWN

Ezra is a thief, a con artist, a pickpocket, and a whiny teen, and three of those things are even USEFUL in some way! So while Boba might charge at him fully armed, Ezra will make sure that in the blink of an eye, Boba's missing his EE-3 carbine rifle, his grenades, and his cape.

HOMEWORLD: KAMINO, PLANET OF "ONE SIZE FITS ALL"

AFFILIATION: BOUNTY HUNTERS (AND KAMINO HIGH SCHOOL SAFETY PATROL)

SPECIES: HUMAN CLONE (NOT TO BE CONFUSED WITH HUMAN CLOWN)

WEAPON: EE-3 CARBINE RIFLE

SPECIAL MOVE: PISTOL WHIP, AND FALLING INTO LARGE PITS.

STATS

- INTELLIGENCE
- STRENGTH
- AGILITY
- DAMAGE
- CONTROL
- COURAGE
- VENGEANCE-WANTING

WICKET W. WARRICK VS. MAX REBO

It's Wicket, the dependable scout who was the first Ewok to befriend the rebels, versus . . . a guy in a band. So you may scoff at the idea of such a tiny warrior facing off against a formidable-looking foe, but keep in mind that he's really just . . . some guy in a band. Also, Wicket REALLY knows his way around a spear.

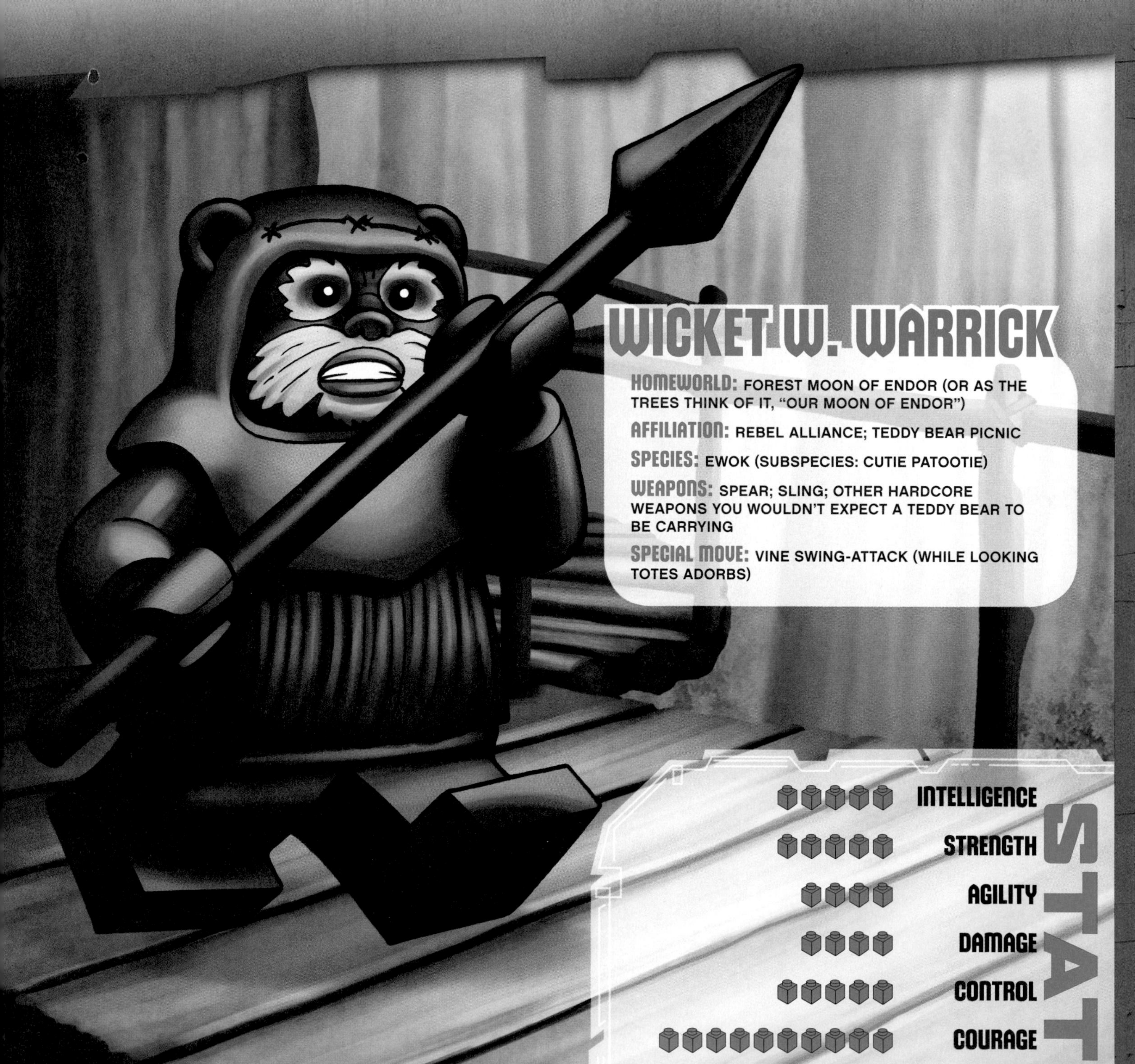

WICKET W. WARRICK

HOMEWORLD: FOREST MOON OF ENDOR (OR AS THE TREES THINK OF IT, "OUR MOON OF ENDOR")

AFFILIATION: REBEL ALLIANCE; TEDDY BEAR PICNIC

SPECIES: EWOK (SUBSPECIES: CUTIE PATOOTIE)

WEAPONS: SPEAR; SLING; OTHER HARDCORE WEAPONS YOU WOULDN'T EXPECT A TEDDY BEAR TO BE CARRYING

SPECIAL MOVE: VINE SWING-ATTACK (WHILE LOOKING TOTES ADORBS)

STATS

Stat	Bricks
INTELLIGENCE	5
STRENGTH	5
AGILITY	4
DAMAGE	4
CONTROL	5
COURAGE	10
CUTE, WIDDLE BELLY BUTTON	10

THE SHOWDOWN

Wicket enters the nightclub expecting to have a relaxing night out. But when Max Rebo tells him that "pets must wait outside," those are fighting words! However, Max Rebo is a veteran of the hardscrabble Tatooine music scene, and has some fighting experience himself. Also, his music is so bad it sometimes CAUSES fights.

HOMEWORLD: ORTO, PLANET OF ELEPHANT-LOOKING PEOPLE WHO ARE NOT ACTUALLY ELEPHANTS

AFFILIATION: MAX REBO BAND (DUH!)

SPECIES: ORTOLAN (WHICH IS A TYPE OF ALIEN, ALTHOUGH IT SOUNDS LIKE A LOW-CALORIE MARGARINE SUBSTITUTE)

WEAPONS: BRUTE STRENGTH; DANGEROUSLY CHEESY POWER BALLADS (HE IS A MUSICIAN, AFTER ALL . . .)

SPECIAL MOVE: SMACKS YOU WHEN YOU OFFER HIM A PEANUT

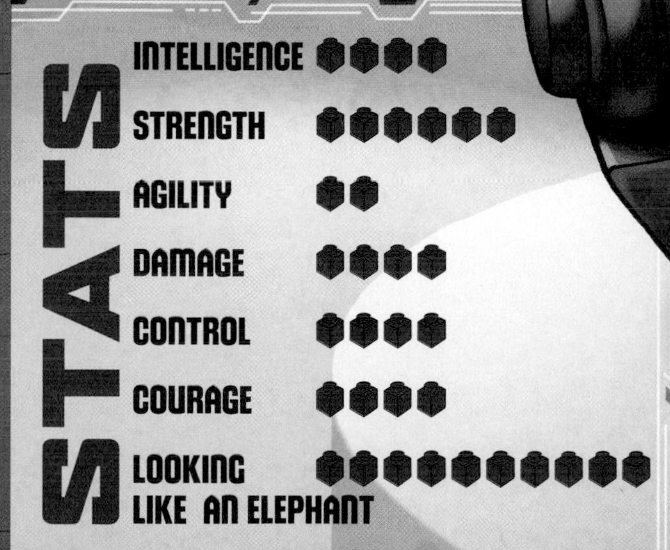

LANDO CALRISSIAN VS. EMPEROR PALPATINE

Well, well, well, what have we here? It's the smoothest, coolest guy in the universe versus . . . the opposite of that. While on a mission for the Rebel Alliance, Lando Calrissian stole some secret files from Emperor Palpatine, and now they find themselves face-to-face. If he can't best the Emperor, maybe Lando can at least steal the old man's false teeth!

LANDO CALRISSIAN

HOMEWORLD: UNKNOWN (PROBABLY SOMEWHERE COOL, THOUGH)

AFFILIATION: REBEL ALLIANCE . . . EVENTUALLY!

SPECIES: HUMAN (SUBSPECIES: THE "SWAGGER" SIDE OF THE FORCE)

WEAPONS: HOLD-OUT BLASTER; RAZOR-SHARP WIT

SPECIAL MOVE: DEAL MAKING

STATS

INTELLIGENCE

STRENGTH

AGILITY

DAMAGE

CONTROL

COURAGE

SMOOTH TALKING

THE SHOWDOWN

Too bad Calrissian's charm won't work on Emperor Palpatine, who looks like a really angry raisin. A raisin who won't be bested by a cool-outfit-haver. But while Lando won't stop Ol' Prune Face by throwing playing cards at him, he does have secret weapons hidden all over himself. Even in his mustache.

HOMEWORLD: NABOO (WHEN HE LAYS THE SMACKDOWN, HE'LL GIVE YOU A "NABOO-BOO!")

AFFILIATION: SITH ORDER; GALACTIC EMPIRE (FOUNDER, EXEC VP IN CHARGE OF TOTALLY CRUSHING IT)

SPECIES: HUMAN (JUST BARELY)

WEAPONS: LIGHTSABER (RED BLADE); HIS FACE (REPULSIVE)

SPECIAL MOVES: FORCE LIGHTNING; LAUGHING EVILLY; NEGLECTING SKIN CARE

PADMÉ NABERRIE VS. STORMTROOPER

Padmé Naberrie, later known as Padmé Amidala, often fought alongside the clone troopers, those nutty guys who all have the same shoe size. But what would happen if she found herself fighting against one of the clone troopers' successors, a (wait for it) STORMtrooper? Would she underestimate him, or would he be distracted by her insanely awesome coolness?

PADMÉ NABERRIE

HOMEWORLD: NABOO (HOME OF GORGEOUS WATERFALLS, LUSH SCENERY, AND—FOR SOME REASON—BRUTAL INVASIONS)

AFFILIATION: GALACTIC REPUBLIC; DECOY-OWNERS SOCIETY

SPECIES: HUMAN (SUBSPECIES: FANCY SHMANCY)

WEAPONS: ELG-3A ROYAL PISTOL; COMPASSIONATE SPEECHES (BUT REALLY, THE PISTOL'S WAY MORE EFFECTIVE)

SPECIAL MOVE: HIDING HER SECRET MARRIAGE

STATS

Stat	Bricks
INTELLIGENCE	8
STRENGTH	6
AGILITY	6
DAMAGE	4
CONTROL	7
COURAGE	10
WEARING FUNNY HEADDRESSES	10

THE SHOWDOWN

The stormtrooper goes on the offensive, but he thinks this means saying offensive THINGS, like "Your clothes are tacky!" While he wastes time trying to think of witty insults, Padmé draws her blaster. To make this a fair fight, she tells her foe to draw his weapon. Nodding, he draws a charcoal sketch of a blaster, and Padmé mutters, "It's going to be a long showdown . . ."

HOMEWORLD: VARIOUS (WHEREVER HIRED GOONS COME FROM)

AFFILIATION: GALACTIC EMPIRE; HIRED GOONS GUILD

SPECIES: VARIOUS (BASICALLY, WHATEVER SPECIES CAN COMFORTABLY FIT INTO THAT ARMOR)

WEAPONS: E-11 BLASTER RIFLE; DLT-19 HEAVY BLASTER RIFLE; POW-POW INSANELY HUGE BLASTER RIFLE

SPECIAL MOVE: NOT BEING ABLE TO SHOOT STRAIGHT

STATS

INTELLIGENCE

STRENGTH

AGILITY

DAMAGE

CONTROL

COURAGE

BAD MARKSMANSHIP

KI-ADI-MUNDI VS. ASAJJ VENTRESS

Jedi Master Ki-Adi-Mundi has confronted dark side warrior Asajj Ventress, someone who really needs to take the "intensity" thing down a notch or two. Jedi and warrior are locked in combat, but who will win? It's the big, bald-looking head versus the regular-sized bald head. One thing's for sure: Neither of them ever needs a haircut!

HOMEWORLD: CEREA (PLANET OF DUDES WITH BIG HEADS)

AFFILIATION: JEDI ORDER; "DUDES WITH BIG HEADS" CLUB

SPECIES: CEREAN (DUDES WITH BIG HEADS)

WEAPONS: LIGHTSABER (BLUE BLADE); ALL THE BIG KNOWLEDGE IN HIS BIG HEAD

SPECIAL MOVES: RAMMING HIS BIG HEAD INTO THINGS (PROBABLY AT SOME POINT, RIGHT?)

STATS

INTELLIGENCE

STRENGTH

AGILITY

DAMAGE

CONTROL

COURAGE

GETTING A "SWELLED HEAD" WHEN HE'S RIGHT ABOUT SOMETHING

THE SHOWDOWN

Ventress attempts to distract Mundi by joining her lightsabers end-to-end and forming a double-sided weapon, which makes it look like the most deadly marching band baton EVER. But the Cerean Jedi refuses to be rattled, and as Ventress darts toward him, Mundi shows how chill he is by using his fiery lightsaber blade to ROAST MARSHMALLOWS, Y'ALL.

ASAJJ VENTRESS

HOMEWORLD: DATHOMIR, WHERE APPARENTLY NOBODY SMILES. LIKE EVER.

AFFILIATION: SEPARATIST ALLIANCE; NIGHTSISTERS COVEN "SITH LORD WANNABES" SOCIETY

SPECIES: DATHOMIRIAN (SUBSPECIES: POUTY FACE)

WEAPONS: TWIN LIGHTSABERS (RED BLADES); STINK-EYE (WHICH SHE GIVES TO, WELL, EVERYONE)

SPECIAL MOVES: FORCE CHOKE; AND THE LESS WELL-KNOWN "FORCE-CAUSED NASAL CONGESTION"

STATS

Stat	Rating
INTELLIGENCE	6 bricks
STRENGTH	7 bricks
AGILITY	8 bricks
DAMAGE	9 bricks
CONTROL	7 bricks
COURAGE	9 bricks
"SINISTER" POSES	10 bricks

R2-D2 & C-3PO VS. JABBA THE HUTT

R2-D2 and C-3PO have downloaded Jabba the Hutt's private diary, and Jabba is frightened that the droids might tell everyone Jabba's most embarrassing secrets. It's the silicon-based synthetics vs. the slimy space slug!

R2-D2 & C-3PO

R2-D2:

HOMEWORLD: NABOO (OR AS R2-D2 CALLS IT, "BWOOOO-BEEEP!")

AFFILIATION: GALACTIC REPUBLIC; WHISTLING AND BEEPING CLUB; ROBOTS WHO ARE FREQUENTLY MISTAKEN FOR TRASH CANS

C-3PO:

WEAPON: ABILITY TO ANNOY YOU TO DEATH (WELL, NOT REALLY)

SPECIAL MOVE: CAN DESCRIBE COOL THINGS OTHER, MORE HEROIC CHARACTERS ARE DOING . . . IN OVER SIX MILLION FORMS OF COMMUNICATION

STATS

INTELLIGENCE

STRENGTH

AGILITY

DAMAGE

CONTROL

COURAGE

ABILITY TO GET TAKEN APART AND PUT BACK TOGETHER AGAIN

THE SHOWDOWN

The sluglike Jabba backs the droids into a corner. R2-D2 fires up his rocket boosters and flies off, taking C-3PO WITH him. But Jabba knocks them to the ground with his tail. Will Jabba tear up the droids? Does R2-D2 have a can of "Hutt repellent" in his weapons' stash?

FULL NAME: JABBA DESILIJIC TIURE (OR "GARY," FOR SHORT)

HOMEWORLD: NAL HUTTA (WHERE HE'S ACTUALLY CONSIDERED IN GOOD SHAPE)

AFFILIATION: DESILIJIC KAJIDIC (A HUTT CLAN THAT BELIEVES IN FEAR, INTIMIDATION, AND CREAMY DESSERTS)

SPECIES: HUTT (VOTED "SLIMIEST SPECIES ALIVE" BY SLIME MAGAZINE)

WEAPONS: DOES HE REALLY NEED ANY?

SPECIAL MOVES: EATING STUFF; KILLING STUFF; GETTING HIS WAY . . . OR ELSE

STATS

INTELLIGENCE

STRENGTH

AGILITY

DAMAGE

CONTROL

COURAGE

CONSUMPTION OF INTERGALACTIC "ALL YOU CAN EAT" BUFFETS

POE DAMERON VS. SAVAGE OPRESS

Poe Dameron is the most heroic X-wing pilot in the galaxy. Savage Oppress can't even SPELL "heroic." Opress might be a powerful fighter, but can he stand up to Poe Dameron's super positive attitude?

POE DAMERON

HOMEWORLD: YAVIN 4, A MOON COVERED IN JUNGLE FOLIAGE (AND DESPERATELY IN NEED OF A DECENT HEDGE-CLIPPER)

AFFILIATION: NEW REPUBLIC; RESISTANCE; COOL-JACKET-WEARERS SOCIETY

SPECIES: HUMAN (SUBSPECIES: GUYS WHO LOOK GOOD IN ORANGE)

WEAPON: RESISTANCE BLASTECH EL-16 HFE BLASTER RIFLE (IT BLASTS THE NEGATIVITY AWAY!)

SPECIAL MOVES: SUCCESSFULLY PILOTING ANYTHING WITH WINGS (EXCEPT MAYBE A DUCK); ESCAPING CERTAIN DEATH (WELL, THAT WOULD MAKE IT "NOT-SO-CERTAIN DEATH," WOULDN'T IT?)

STATS

Bricks	Stat
6	INTELLIGENCE
7	STRENGTH
5	AGILITY
6	DAMAGE
7	CONTROL
10	COURAGE
10	SKILLED PILOT AND ACCOMPLISHED SOLDIER

THE SHOWDOWN

Savage Opress jumps atop the hood of Dameron's X-wing while the vehicle is taking off, intending to destroy his foe in mid-flight. But Opress didn't count on one thing: Poe getting off the ground. Hold on, because it's going to be a wild ride!

HOMEWORLD: DATHOMIR (A PLANET WHERE "PROFESSIONAL HORN-SHARPENER" IS AN ACTUAL PROFESSION)

AFFILIATION: SITH ORDER; "DISARRAY AND DISORDER" ORDER

SPECIES: DATHOMIRIAN ZABRAK (SUBSPECIES: BIG BROTHERS OF BIG VILLAINS)

WEAPONS: DOUBLE-ENDED LIGHTSABER; SINGLE-ENDED HORNS

SPECIAL MOVES: FORCE SLAM; BODY SLAM; SLAM DUNK (HE'S GOOD AT BASKETBALL, OKAY?)

STATS

INTELLIGENCE	■■■■■
STRENGTH	■■■■■■■■■
AGILITY	■■■■■
DAMAGE	■■■■■■■■■
CONTROL	■■■■■■■
COURAGE	■■■■■■■
CONTINUALLY LIVING IN THE SHADOW OF HIS KID BROTHER, DARTH MAUL	■■■■■■■■■■

BB-8 VS. TUSKEN RAIDER

BB-8 encounters what APPEARS to be TS-6, a droid the friendly astromech knew back in high school, but our hero discovers that "TS-6" is just . . . a toaster. Well, not just any toaster. It's a toaster belonging to a fearsome Tusken Raider! And BB-8 has disturbed the Raider's slumber, so the Raider in question challenges BB-8 to a brawl. It's beeping BB versus the roaring Raider!

BB-8

HOMEWORLD: UNKNOWN (BUT BB-8 IS ROUND, SO MAYBE IT COMES FROM ONE OF THOSE ROUND PLANETS)

AFFILIATION: NEW REPUBLIC; RESISTANCE; "SHAPED LIKE A SNOWMAN" SOCIETY

MANUFACTURER: UNKNOWN

DROID TYPE: ASTROMECH DROID (SUB-CATEGORY: ROLY-POLY)

WEAPONS: RETRACTABLE WELDING TORCH; ROLLING ITSELF OVER BAD GUYS LIKE A BOWLING BALL

STATS

Stat	Bricks
INTELLIGENCE	5
STRENGTH	3
AGILITY	5
DAMAGE	3
CONTROL	5
COURAGE	6
ABILITY TO HIDE IMPORTANT STUFF	10

THE SHOWDOWN

The ruthless Tusken Raider, furious at having been awakened from a dream in which he was in a rainbow castle with gumdrop waterfalls, advances on BB-8. But the nimble astromech droid is not without its resources, and it uses its ball-like body to PUNT its adversary in the stomach! The terrifying Tusken Raider keels over, but will he remain down for the count?

HOMEWORLD: TATOOINE, WHERE EVERYONE WEARS SUNBLOCK. LIKE, ALWAYS.

SPECIES: TUSKEN (CONSISTENTLY VOTED "MOST OVERDRESSED")

AFFILIATION: NONE (THEY'RE NOT EXACTLY WHAT YOU'D CALL "SOCIABLE")

WEAPONS: GADERFFII (GAFFI) STICK; SNIPER RIFLE; BEACH BALL

SPECIAL MOVES: TUSKEN TROUNCE; KICKING SAND IN YOUR FACE

STATS

INTELLIGENCE	●●●●●
STRENGTH	●●●●●●●●
AGILITY	●●●●
DAMAGE	●●●●●●
CONTROL	●●●●●●
COURAGE	●●●●●●
RAISING THEIR STAFFS ABOVE THEIR HEADS MENACINGLY	●●●●●●●●●●

REY VS. RANCOR

She's a plucky gearhead and a true self-starter. He's a hideous monster. She's a scavenger of great resourcefulness and bravery. He's . . . a hideous monster. But what if Rey found herself facing off against the fearsome rancor, a creature who has clearly NEVER heard of showering or underarm deodorant?

THE SHOWDOWN

The rancor lets out a piercing battle cry and lashes out at Rey with his razor-sharp claws. But the monster's fighting technique is as sloppy and funky as cafeteria meatloaf. Rey's fighting style, by contrast, is graceful, satisfying, and balanced, like a fancy filet mignon. So even though she's much smaller than her opponent, Rey might just win this melee.

HOMEWORLD: ALLEGEDLY DATHOMIR (A PLANET SO SCARY, RANCORS ARE CONSIDERED CUDDLY)

AFFILIATION: "PIT DWELLERS" UNION

SPECIES: RANCOR (SUBSPECIES: CRANKY)

WEAPONS: HIS FANGS, CLAWS, AND GENERAL ENORMOUSNESS

SPECIAL MOVES: BOULDER TOSS; PERSON TOSS; COIN TOSS

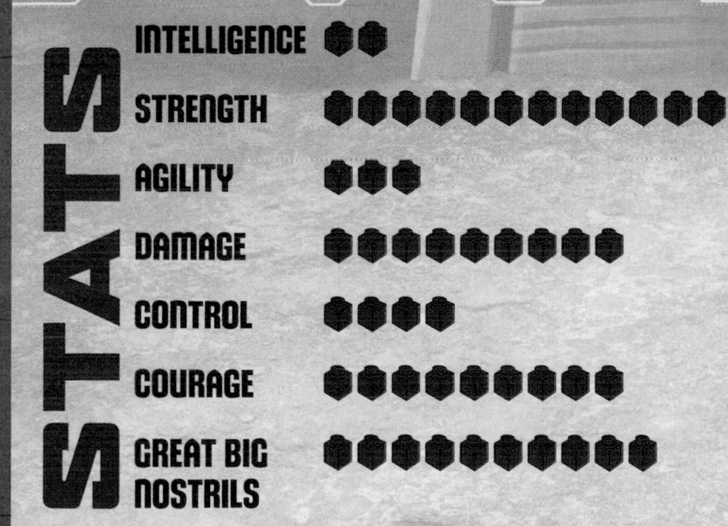

YODA VS. DARTH VADER

Way back when Darth Vader was still Anakin Skywalker, he and Yoda went together like Jedi and humorlessness! All that ended when Yoda went into hiding in a super disgusting swamp and Anakin became Darth Vader, the wheeziest supervillain in the galaxy! But what if Yoda came out of his rustic retirement to lay the swampy smackdown on Darth Whooping Cough?

THE SHOWDOWN

Darth Vader is . . . not as fast as he was before he was a hulking, semi-robotic monstrosity. And Yoda's not as sprightly as HE was back before the Jedi Order was destroyed and his life became one huge bummer. So what you're looking at is two old dudes who will probably need to take a "time-out" every now and then. Maybe even a nap.

DARTH VADER

HOMEWORLD: TATOOINE (HUMAN BODY PARTS); ED'S BODY SHOP AND GARAGE (CYBERNETIC BODY PARTS)

AFFILIATION: SITH ORDER; GALACTIC EMPIRE; PROFESSIONAL "FORCE PUSHERS" UNION

SPECIES: HUMAN (PARTIALLY); SOME KIND OF ROBOT-THINGY (MOSTLY)

WEAPONS: LIGHTSABER (RED BLADE); HEAVYSABER (WHAT, YOU DIDN'T KNOW ABOUT THE HEAVYSABER? AWWW, JUST KIDDIN'.)

SPECIAL MOVE: SABER THROW (ESPECIALLY HELPFUL WHEN USING LIGHTSABER TO PLAY DARTS)

STATS

Stat	Rating (bricks)
INTELLIGENCE	7
STRENGTH	10
AGILITY	4
DAMAGE	8
CONTROL	8
COURAGE	8
OBVIOUS HEALTH ISSUES (WHEEZING, HEAVY BREATHING, ETC)	10

JEDI LUKE VS. GENERAL GRIEVOUS

General Grievous was turned into evil-guy scrap metal before Luke was even BORN. BUT what if things had played out differently? What if the wheezing cyborg bad guy that Luke had to fight in an epic battle was not Darth Vader, but rather (*dum dum dum*) GENERAL GRIEVOUS?

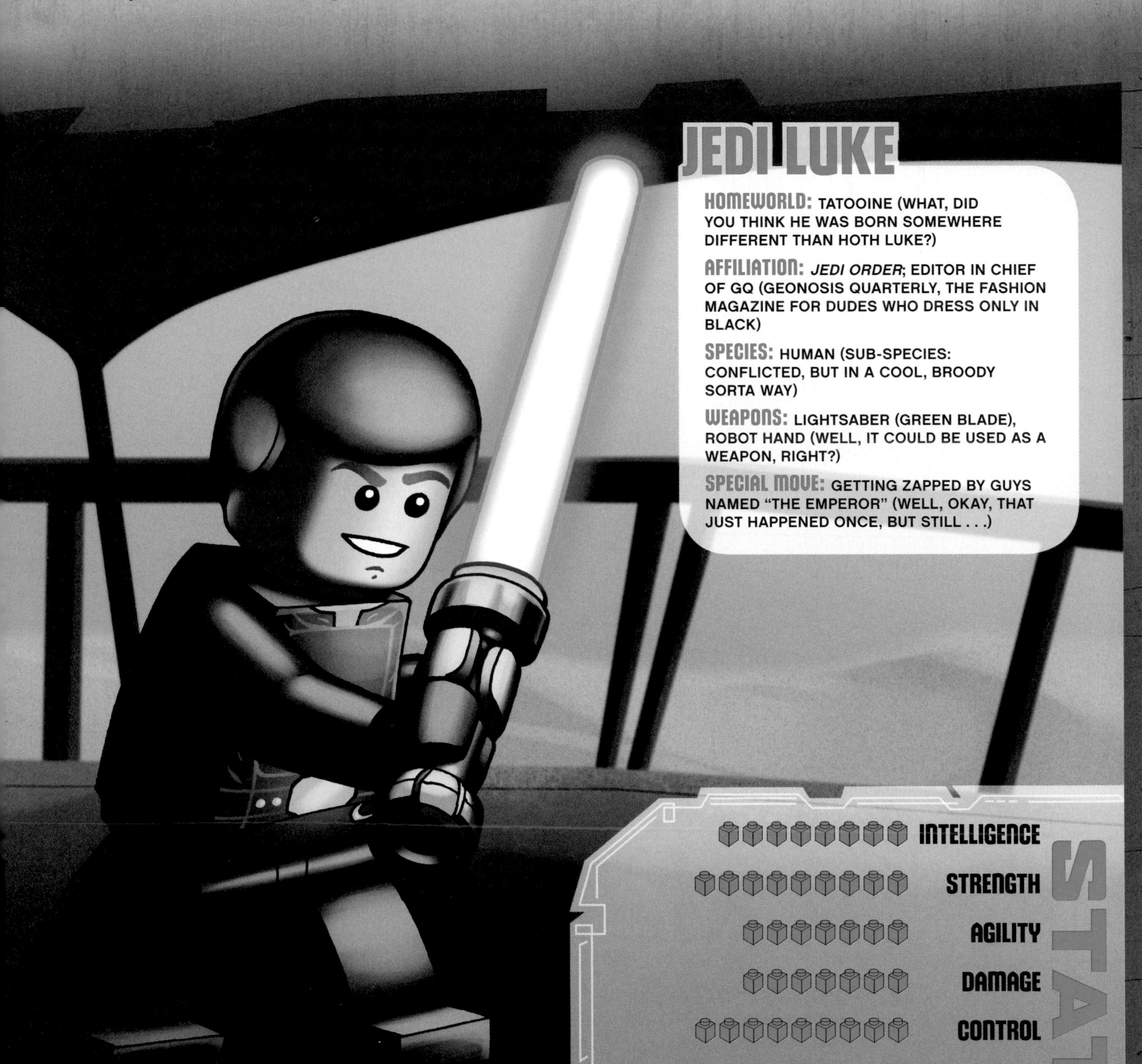

THE SHOWDOWN

With his four robo-arms spinning colorful lightsabers, Grievous looks like a deadly windmill. With a hacking cough. And Skywalker may be less experienced than his cyborg foe, but unlike Grievous, Luke is BFFs with a couple of GGJ (Glowy Ghost Jedi).

ADMIRAL ACKBAR VS. BIB FORTUNA

While on a mission to "steal back" all the donuts Jabba the Hutt plundered from the Rebellion, Admiral Ackbar comes across Jabba's lackey Bib Fortuna. Before the admiral can yell, "It's a trap!" he's under attack! As Bib Fortuna rushes Admiral Ackbar, the fearsome Twi'lek bares the fangs that earned him the childhood nickname "Bitey McGee."

ADMIRAL ACKBAR

HOMEWORLD: MON CALA (AKA FOLKS WITH EXCELLENT PERIPHERAL VISION)

AFFILIATION: REBEL ALLIANCE; THE "WE ARE NOT SEAFOOD" SOCIETY

SPECIES: MON CALAMARI (THEY HATE BEING MISTAKEN FOR SQUIDS)

WEAPONS: BATON/BLASTER; ABILITY TO IMPERSONATE A SQUID (BUT ONLY IF YOU ABSOLUTELY NEED HIM TO)

SPECIAL MOVE: MAKING EVERYONE WHO LOOKS AT HIM INSTANTLY CRAVE SEAFOOD

STATS

INTELLIGENCE

STRENGTH

AGILITY

DAMAGE

CONTROL

COURAGE

GRUFF "AUTHORITY FIGURE" VOICE

THE SHOWDOWN

Not wanting to get Twi'lek drool on his clothes, Ackbar draws his blaster and aims it at Fortuna's pretzel-like head-tails. Bib Fortuna yells, "Hands off my handsome, distinguished head-tails!" But he says it in his native tongue. Admiral Ackbar doesn't understand and all he can think is, "It's a trap!"

BIB FORTUNA

HOMEWORLD: RYLOTH (WHOSE INHABITANTS EAT FUNGI AND MOLDS. WHAT'S THE MATTER? LOSE YOUR APPETITE?)

AFFILIATION: JABBA THE HUTT'S CRIMINAL EMPIRE; TWI'LEK CLAN COUNCIL; AUTHOR OF THE TWI'LEK SAGA SERIES OF YOUNG ADULT NOVELS

SPECIES: TWI'LEK (YOU KNOW, THE FOLKS WITH THE TAILS GROWING OUT OF THEIR HEADS)

WEAPONS: FANGS; POCKETS FULL OF FUNGI AND MOLDS

SPECIAL MOVES: GETTING TOTALLY OWNED BY LUKE SKYWALKER; BRAGGING ABOUT HOW HE EATS FUNGI AND MOLDS; WAVING HELLO WITH HIS BRAIN-TAILS

STATS

INTELLIGENCE

STRENGTH

AGILITY

DAMAGE

CONTROL

COURAGE

LOOKING LIKE HE'S WEARING A WORM HAT

FINN VS. DARTH MALGUS

Finn is a former stormtrooper who decided that evil was for chumps. Darth Malgus is a Sith Lord who decided that evil was for CHAMPS. Finn is devoted to his friends, and Malgus is devoted to fiends. If they fought, would Finn win or would he get floored by this Sith Lord?

HOMEWORLD: UNKNOWN (BUT OBVIOUSLY ONE OF THOSE PLANETS WHERE PEOPLE WHO CAN FIT INTO STORMTROOPER ARMOR ARE BORN)

AFFILIATION: FIRST ORDER; RESISTANCE; RETIRED STORMTROOPER SOCIETY; CAPTAIN PHASMA NONFAN CLUB.

SPECIES: HUMAN (SUBSPECIES: UNINTENTIONAL HERO)

WEAPON: RESISTANCE BLASTECH EL-16 HFE BLASTER RIFLE (AND THE "HFE" DEFINITELY DOESN'T STAND FOR "HUGS FOREVER")

SPECIAL MOVE: CALLING HIMSELF A "BIG DEAL"

STATS

INTELLIGENCE

STRENGTH

AGILITY

DAMAGE

CONTROL

COURAGE

"BORROWING" LIGHTSABERS

THE SHOWDOWN

As Finn stares down his foe, he mutters, "Y'know, Darth Malgus, if you wore a turtleneck, you would look less like a weirdo!" But before Finn can give him any MORE unsolicited fashion advice, the imposing Sith Lord runs toward him, lightsaber at the ready.

DARTH MALGUS

HOMEWORLD: DROMUND KAAS, CAPITAL OF THE SITH EMPIRE (A REAL "GLASS HALF EMPTY" KINDA PLACE)

AFFILIATION: SITH ORDER; "GUYS WHO ARE KIND OF LIKE DARTH VADER BUT NOT ACTUALLY DARTH VADER" SOCIETY

SPECIES: HUMAN (SUBSPECIES: BIG OL' GRUMP)

WEAPONS: HIS FACE (ALSO, HIS LIGHTSABER . . . BUT REALLY, THAT FACE! YECCCH!)

SPECIAL MOVES: FORCE PUSH, FORCE JUMP, FORCE JUMP-ROPE

STATS

INTELLIGENCE

STRENGTH

AGILITY

DAMAGE

CONTROL

COURAGE

HEAD THAT LOOKS LIKE A SOFT-BOILED EGG

PONG KRELL VS. CAPTAIN PHASMA

Pong Krell is a grumpy Jedi who is as nice as he is handsome. Captain Phasma is a big important First Order mucky-muck who insists that her stormtroopers are orderly and efficient, and that their armor has that "new armor smell." But what if these two soldiers met in battle?

THE SHOWDOWN

Captain Phasma fires several perfectly aimed shots at Pong Krell, who blocks ALL of the incoming blasts with his four lightsabers. Phasma vows to get as close as she can to defeat him. But, being a perfectionist, she also worries about whether she remembered to turn the oven off!

CAPTAIN PHASMA

HOMEWORLD: UNKNOWN

AFFILIATION: FIRST ORDER; PERFECTIONIST SOCIETY

SPECIES: HUMAN

WEAPONS: CHROME-FINISHED SONN-BLAS F-11D BLASTER RIFLE; DISAPPROVING ATTITUDE

SPECIAL MOVES: PATROLLING HALLWAYS IN SLO-MO WHILE MOODY MUSIC PLAYS IN THE BACKGROUND

STATS

INTELLIGENCE	8
STRENGTH	9
AGILITY	7
DAMAGE	7
CONTROL	10
COURAGE	6
BRUSHED CHROMIUM ARMOR, MARTIAL ARTS	10

MACE WINDU VS. KYLO REN

Both of these guys take themselves super-seriously. Maybe a little too seriously. You definitely get the sense that neither of these guys has ever put on some swim trunks and run through the lawn sprinkler on a hot summer day. But what if these ultra-serious dudes were to do battle? Whoever wins will run through the lawn sprinkler of victory.

MACE WINDU

HOMEWORLD: HOMEWORLD: HARUUN KAL (BUT BASED ON HIS ATTITUDE, HE SEEMS TO BE FROM "STUBBORN-TOWN")

AFFILIATION: JEDI ORDER; "PEOPLE WHO LIKE THINGS IN A CERTAIN ORDER" ORDER

SPECIES: HUMAN (SUBSPECIES: HUMORLESS HUMAN)

WEAPONS: LIGHTSABER (PURPLE BLADE); JEDI ARMOR (HE LIKES TO PRETEND IT'S PURPLE)

SPECIAL MOVES: BEHIND-THE-BACK PARRY AND STRIKE: FORCE WAVE; FORCE "WAVE HELLO;" DEADLY SERIOUSNESS

STATS

INTELLIGENCE

STRENGTH

AGILITY

DAMAGE

CONTROL

COURAGE

HAVING A PURPLE LIGHTSABER

THE SHOWDOWN

With his black cloak, Kylo Ren silently disappears into the shadows. But Mace Windu concentrates, sensing Ren's presence the same way he would sense a dirty sock that desperately needed washing. Lashing out, Ren swats at Mace Windu like one would swat at a bee. But if Mace is a bee, his purple lightsaber is gonna deliver such a sting . . . .

KYLO REN

HOMEWORLD: UNKNOWN

AFFILIATION: FIRST ORDER; COOL BAD GUY GUILD; BETRAYAL SOCIETY

SPECIES: HUMAN (NOT THAT YOU CAN TELL WHEN HE'S WEARING THAT BIG OL' MASK)

WEAPON: CROSS-HILT LIGHTSABER (CUSTOM-BUILT)

SPECIAL MOVE: TALKING TO AN ENORMOUS HOLOGRAM OF HIS BOSS

STATS

INTELLIGENCE

STRENGTH

AGILITY

DAMAGE

CONTROL

COURAGE

FIERY TEMPER

PLO KOON VS. TASU LEECH

Always eager to enforce the law, Plo Koon has arrived to serve Tasu Leech a parking ticket for illegally docking his ship. Tasu has already been served a speeding ticket by different Jedi, and this is his chance to get revenge. Firing wildly at the masked Jedi, Tasu hopes to win the day, not realizing that Plo is writing him another ticket for "illegally firing wildly."

PLO KOON

HOMEWORLD: DORIN (WHERE THE WEATHER IS WINDY, BUT NOT *MACE* WINDY)

AFFILIATION: JEDI ORDER; GUYS WHO CONSIDER SUNGLASSES REDUNDANT

SPECIES: KEL DOR (AKA "THE FOLKS WHO USE THOSE BREATHING-MASK THINGIES")

WEAPONS: LIGHTSABER (BLUE BLADE); HAS A THICK SKIN (PHYSICALLY, NOT EMOTIONALLY)

SPECIAL MOVES: ARMORED TALON SLAP; USING HIS ARMORED TALONS AS A BACK-SCRATCHER

STATS

INTELLIGENCE

STRENGTH

AGILITY

DAMAGE

CONTROL

COURAGE

LOOKING COOL WEARING GOGGLES

THE SHOWDOWN

Plo Koon orders Tasu to stand down, or at least to sit down or possibly to take a nap, since the gangster is clearly very cranky. But Tasu is not going to take a nap. For one thing, Kanjiklub gang bosses don't back down. For another, he just woke up from a nap. "Uh-oh," Plo thinks as Tasu reloads his blaster rifle, "If he's fully rested, perhaps I am in trouble . . . "

TASU LEECH

HOMEWORLD: NAR KANJI (HE'S A FREQUENT STAR OF THE TRUE CRIME TV SHOW "LAW & ORDER: NAR KANJI")

AFFILIATION: KANJIKLUB; RACQUETBALL KLUB; "HAN SOLO STINKS" SOCIETY

SPECIES: HUMAN (SUBSPECIES: SUPER SLEAZY)

WEAPONS: HUTTSPLITTER OVERPOWER BLASTER RIFLE WITH VIBRO-SPIKE BAYONET; MUSTACHE TRIMMER (TECHNICALLY NOT A WEAPON, BUT A NEATLY TRIMMED GANGSTER IS A SUCCESSFUL GANGSTER)

SPECIAL MOVE: RUNNING AWAY FROM A RATHTAR WHILE IT EATS HIS FLUNKIES

STATS

INTELLIGENCE

STRENGTH

AGILITY

DAMAGE

CONTROL

COURAGE

STREET FIGHTER, REFUSES TO SPEAK BASIC

ANAKIN'S JEDI STARFIGHTER VS. KYLO REN'S COMMAND SHUTTLE

These two vehicles are from two very different eras in galactic history, but what if they squared off? While Anakin's starfighter is faster, Kylo Ren's command shuttle is . . . um . . . better at transporting stuff. Which is totally useless in a battle like this . . .

ANAKIN'S JEDI STARFIGHTER

MANUFACTURER: KUAT SYSTEMS ENGINEERING (MOTTO: "WHEN YOU NEED SYSTEMS TO BE ENGINEERED, UM . . . WE'LL DO THAT")

AFFILIATION: JEDI ORDER; "MACHINES THAT AREN'T SENTIENT ROBOTS" TYPE: MODIFIED DELTA-B AETHERSPRITE LIGHT INTERCEPTOR (GOOD FOR INTERCEPTING STUFF, LIKE ENEMY SHIPS, VITAL TRANSMISSIONS, AND TASTY CUPCAKES)

WEAPONS: 2 LASER CANNONS (CONTRARY TO POPULAR BELIEF, THEY DON'T SHOOT "LASER CANNONBALLS")

TOP SPEED: 1,260 KPH (IN ATMOSPHERE)

STATS

Stat	Bricks
CONTROL	7
HULL	6
MANEUVER	8
SPEED	8
FIREPOWER	5
AWESOME YELLOW PAINT JOB	10

THE SHOWDOWN

. . . Unless Kylo Ren's crew decides to dump its cargo on the starfighter in a totally desperate, last-ditch move . . . Which it does! Will Anakin dig himself out from under twenty crates of military-grade First Order hot cocoa? Or will he simply . . . drink the cocoa?

MANUFACTURER: SIENAR-JAEMUS FLEET SYSTEMS

AFFILIATION: FIRST ORDER

TYPE: UPSILON-CLASS COMMAND SHUTTLE

SIZE: 37.2 METERS (NOT COUNTING THE GINORMOUS BLASTERS IN FRONT!)

WEAPONS: TWIN HEAVY LASER CANNONS

TOP SPEED: AS FAST AS KYLO REN DARN WELL PLEASES

STATS

- CONTROL ●●●●●●
- HULL ●●●●●
- MANEUVER ●●●●
- SPEED ●●●●●
- FIREPOWER ●●●●
- LOOKING SUPER SWEET ●●●●●●●●●

WOOKIEE GUNSHIP VS. FIRST ORDER SPECIAL FORCES TIE FIGHTER

One is a high-tech vessel used by evil people to carry out evil tasks. The other is so low-tech it's partially made from trees, but it's not at all evil. (Unless it was made from evil trees, which it isn't.) How would these two signature ships measure up against each other?

WOOKIEE GUNSHIP

MANUFACTURER: APPAZANNA ENGINEERING WORKS, A WOOKIEE-OWNED COMPANY (MOTTO: "ROARRRRR!")

AFFILIATION: REBEL ALLIANCE; WOOKIEES; BASICALLY ANYONE WHO ISN'T A PAWN OF THE EMPEROR

TYPE: AUZITUCK ANTI-SLAVER GUNSHIP (IT'S MADE FROM TREES, SO DON'T FLY IT INTO ANY PLANETS WITH TERMITES)

WEAPONS: 3 SUREGGI LASER CANNONS; STASH OF BOWCASTERS; OTHER WEAPONS WOOKIEES WILL USE IF YOU CALL THEM "WALKING CARPETS"

TOP SPEED: 950 KM/H (WHICH, SINCE WE'RE TALKING ABOUT WOOKIEES, STANDS FOR "KILOMETERS PER HOWL")

STATS

CONTROL

HULL

MANEUVER

SPEED

FIREPOWER

QUALITY RED CARPET (TO BE ROLLED OUT IN THE EVENT THAT WOOKIEE VIP CHEWBACCA COMES ON BOARD)

THE SHOWDOWN

The Wookiee gunship doesn't have the high-tech weaponry of the TIE fighter, which has more bells and whistles than a bells and whistles store. But the gunship just needs one clear shot to win the day, and it's up to each vehicle's pilot to avoid being turned into bantha fodder.

FIRST ORDER SPECIAL FORCES TIE FIGHTER

MANUFACTURER: SIENAR-JAEMUS FLEET SYSTEMS (MOTTO: "SIENAR-JAEMUS: WHEN YOU NEED THAT SWEET FLEET TO BE COMPLETE AND MAKE YOUR FOES BEAT A HASTY RETREAT!")

AFFILIATION: FIRST ORDER; FIRST ORDER MEMBERS WHO FOLLOW ORDERS (GIVEN BY OTHER, MORE-ORDERLY MEMBERS OF THE FIRST ORDER)

TYPE: TIE/SF SPACE SUPERIORITY FIGHTER (IRONICALLY, A PILOT IN A SUPERIORITY FIGHTER USUALLY HAS AN INFERIORITY COMPLEX)

WEAPONS: TWO LASER CANNONS; DUAL HEAVY LASER TURRET; CONCUSSION MISSILES; MAG-PULSE WARHEAD LAUNCHER; "PEACE-HEAD" LAUNCHER.

TOP SPEED: 1,150 KPH (IN ATMOSPHERE); 9,240 KPH (WHEN HURTLING TOWARD THE PLANET JAKKU WHILE ENGULFED IN FLAMES)

STATS

Stat	Rating (bricks)
CONTROL	6
HULL	5
MANEUVER	6
SPEED	6
FIREPOWER	10
ABILITY TO GET TOTALLY TROUNCED BY X-WING FIGHTERS	10

POE'S X-WING VS. SITH INFILTRATOR

Two sleek, stealthy vessels. Both ships have long noses, and both would look super funny if you somehow put a gigantic mustache below those noses. But that's not important right now. What is important is this: who will survive if these two ships went nose to nose — er, head to head?

POE'S X-WING

MANUFACTURER: INCOM-FREITEK (WHICH ALSO MAKES "FRY-TECH," IN OTHER WORDS, MACHINES THAT MANUFACTURE FRENCH FRIES, WAFFLE FRIES, HOME FRIES, AND MORE!)

AFFILIATION: RESISTANCE; LEAGUE OF VEHICLES SHAPED LIKE LETTERS OF THE ALPHABET

TYPE: RESISTANCE T-70 X-WING SPACE SUPERIORITY FIGHTER (THOUGH IT'S UNCLEAR WHETHER THIS MEANS THAT THE FIGHTER IS SUPERIOR OR THAT SPACE IS SUPERIOR)

WEAPONS: 4 LASER CANNONS; 2 PROTON TORPEDO LAUNCHERS; JAR OF LEFTOVER PROTONS TO PUT IN THE PROTON TORPEDOES

TOP SPEED: 1,300 KPH (IN ATMOSPHERE); 40,000 KPH (WHEN ZOOMING AROUND ON TOP-SECRET MISSIONS FOR THE RESISTANCE)

STATS

Bricks	Stat
7	CONTROL
9	HULL
7	MANEUVER
8	SPEED
8	FIREPOWER
10	REFINED ENGINES, CUSTOMIZABLE WEAPONS SYSTEMS

THE SHOWDOWN

Poe, ever-confident and cunning, decides to park his ship and go over his strategy for the battle. But he doesn't realize that he's actually parked ON TOP OF the Sith Infiltrator, which is INVISIBLE. Has Poe's X-wing SQUASHED Darth Maul's Infiltrator for good?

SITH INFILTRATOR

MANUFACTURER: REPUBLIC SIENAR SYSTEMS, CONTRACTED BY DARTH MAUL (MOTTO: "PAY US WHENEVER YOU WANT, DARTH MAUL! WE DON'T MIND WAITING! PLEASE DON'T HURT US!")

AFFILIATION: SITH ORDER; DARTH MAUL APPRECIATION SOCIETY (DARTH MAUL, FOUNDER AND SOLE MEMBER)

TYPE: INFILTRATOR STAR COURIER; DARTH MAUL'S PERSONAL PUNISHMENT-BRINGER

WEAPONS: 6 CONCEALED LASER CANNONS; UNCONCEALED EVIL

TOP SPEED: 1,180 KPH (IN ATMOSPHERE); EVEN FASTER WHEN DARTH MAUL YELLS AT IT TO "GO FASTER!"

STATS

CONTROL ●●●●●

HULL ●●●●●●

MANEUVER ●●●●●●●

SPEED ●●●●●●●●

FIREPOWER ●●●●●●●

LIKELIHOOD THAT SHIP ITSELF IS SCARED OF DARTH MAUL ●●●●●●●●●●

REY'S SPEEDER VS. AT-AT

Rey lives in a toppled AT-AT, but what if she jumped in her speeder and FOUGHT an AT-AT? Would she get squashed like a bug, would she bounce back like a kangaroo, or would some other animal-related metaphor be more appropriate?

REY'S SPEEDER

NAME OF VEHICLE: BUMPER

MANUFACTURER: CUSTOM SPECIAL (IN OTHER WORDS, IT WAS MADE BY REY, FOR REY, BUT HEY, IF YOU'RE FRIENDS WITH REY, YOU CAN TAKE IT FOR A SPIN. SHE'S COOL LIKE THAT . . . .)

AFFILIATION: THE LOOSE COLLECTION OF STUFF REY BUILDS IN HER MAKESHIFT HOUSE-TYPE-DWELLING

TYPE: HYBRID SPEEDER/SWOOP (ALTHOUGH IT LOOKS KINDA LIKE AN ELECTRIC RAZOR)

NO WEAPONS: (WELL, OKAY, IT'S "ARMED" WITH GOOD VIBES, BECAUSE IT WAS BUILT BY (WAIT FOR IT) REY!)

TOP SPEED: 450 KPH (IMPRESSIVE, CONSIDERING IT'S MADE OF STUFF REY FOUND IN THE DESERT)

STATS

Stat	Bricks
CONTROL	3
HULL	2
MANEUVER	7
SPEED	5
FIREPOWER	1
SUPER SLEEKNESS	10

THE SHOWDOWN

Rey's speeder can run circles around the AT-AT! The AT-AT walker might not be as fast, but it's SUPER-BIG, and if it should accidentally FALL on Rey's speeder, she'll have not only the fastest, but also the FLATTEST, vehicle on Jakku!

AT-AT

MANUFACTURER: KUAT DRIVE YARDS (OR SHOULD THAT BE "KUAT WALK YARDS," SINCE THE AT-AT IS A WALKER?)

AFFILIATION: GALACTIC EMPIRE; VEHICLES THAT CAN WALK

TYPE: ALL TERRAIN ARMORED TRANSPORT (AKA "THOSE THINGS THAT STRUT AROUND LIKE SASSY DOGS")

WEAPONS: 2 HEAVY LASER CANNONS; 2 MEDIUM BLASTERS; 1 TEENY-TINY MICRO-BLASTER (WELL, OKAY, IT'S A TWIG, BUT IT'S SHAPED LIKE A BLASTER!)

TOP SPEED: 60 KPH (RUNNING); 30 KPH (WALKING); 0 KPH (STANDING AROUND)

STATS

CONTROL	5
HULL	15
MANEUVER	15
SPEED	4
FIREPOWER	10
LIKELIHOOD THAT SOMEONE WILL TIE THE AT-AT'S LEGS TOGETHER AND TRIP IT	10

MILLENNIUM FALCON VS. TIE ADVANCED PROTOTYPE

The skies will quake (or at least wobble a little) as these metal monsters clash! And probably even clash again! Who will win? Han Solo's hodgepodge hunk of junk? Or the Interrogator's vile vehicle of vengeance, villainy, and vegetables?

MILLENNIUM FALCON

MANUFACTURER: CORELLIAN ENGINEERING CORPORATION (MOTTO: "SERVING THE GALAXY SINCE YODA WAS IN DIAPERS!")

AFFILIATION: REBEL ALLIANCE; SMUGGLERS UNION; JUGGLERS UNION (ACCIDENTALLY, AS RESULT OF TYPO)

TYPE: MODIFIED YT-1300 LIGHT FREIGHTER (MODIFIED TO PREVENT WOOKIEE HAIR FROM CLOGGING THE SINK)

WEAPONS: TWO QUAD LASER CANNONS; TWO CONCUSSION MISSILE TUBES; ONE ANTIPERSONNEL BLASTER; TWO DEATH STAR BLOWER-UPPERS

TOP SPEED: 1,050 KPH IN ATMOSPHERE (LIKE HAN SOLO, THIS VEHICLE IS ALWAYS ON THE MOVE.)

STATS

CONTROL

HULL

MANEUVER

SPEED

FIREPOWER

ENDEARING "PATCHWORK" QUALITY

THE SHOWDOWN

The *Falcon* fires ITS laser cannons, which are so rickety they're held together with old bandages and chewing gum. The cannons ZAP the Inquisitor's TIE Advanced. But the Inquisitor rallies, and his vehicle launches missiles at the Corellian freighter.

TIE ADVANCED PROTOTYPE

MANUFACTURER: SIENAR FLEET SYSTEMS (MOTTO: "WE DON'T CARE WHO OUR CLIENTS ARE! EVEN IF THEY'RE CRAZY, EVIL PEOPLE!")

AFFILIATION: GALACTIC EMPIRE; SITH ORDER; PALPATINE TAXICAB & LIMO SERVICE (SOMETHING THE EMPEROR HAS GOING ON THE SIDE)

TYPE: TWIN ION ENGINE ADVANCED X1, STARFIGHTER (BUT THE IGNITION WON'T START UNLESS THE PILOT IS EVIL)

WEAPONS: TWO L-S9.3 LASER CANNONS; 20 CLUSTER MISSILES; 20 CLUSTERS OF GRAPES (OKAY, GRAPES AREN'T WEAPONS, BUT THEY'RE GREAT FOR SNACKING ON WHEN USING THE WEAPONS)

TOP SPEED: 1,200 KM/H (SOURCE: EVILYMPIC GAMES)

STATS

CONTROL

HULL

MANEUVER

SPEED

FIREPOWER

PROMOTES PILOT'S "CREEPY LONER" IMAGE

NABOO STARFIGHTER VS. IMPERIAL STAR DESTROYER

It's the little starfighter that could versus . . . well, a really big ship. Maybe it's no contest. Maybe the Imperial Star Destroyer would finish off the Naboo starfighter like Jabba finishing off a box of cupcakes. But as Yoda would say, "Judge me not by my size . . . ."

NABOO STARFIGHTER

MANUFACTURER: ENGINEERING CORPS (MOTTO: "MAKIN' VESSELS WITHOUT ANY HASSLES!")

AFFILIATION: GALACTIC REPUBLIC; BUREAU OF SPACESHIPS THAT LOOK LIKE PLASTIC TOYS

TYPE: ROYAL STARFIGHTER (AKA "THAT GLEAMING, SHINY SHIP THAT RESEMBLES A FORK")

WEAPONS: TWO LASER CANNONS; TWO PROTON TORPEDO LAUNCHERS (BATTERIES NOT INCLUDED)

TOP SPEED: 1,100 KPH IN ATMOSPHERE

STATS

CONTROL

HULL

MANEUVER

SPEED

FIREPOWER

RESEMBLES GIANT YELLOW HAIR CLIP

THE SHOWDOWN

The Imperial warship bears down on the Naboo starfighter like a floating triangle of doom! And the starfighter might look like a tiny toy sword, but that's mighty appropriate, because it's about to BRING THE PAIN! (Not the TOY pain, the REAL pain!)

IMPERIAL STAR DESTROYER

MANUFACTURER: KUAT DRIVE YARDS (MOTTO: "WE'LL BUILD KUAT-EVER YOU WANT TO DRIVE!")

AFFILIATION: GALACTIC EMPIRE; VEHICLES THAT ARE TOO BIG TO PARK ANYWHERE

TYPE: IMPERIAL STAR DESTROYER (AKA "THAT BIG TRIANGLE-SHAPED MONSTROSITY")

WEAPONS: 60 TURBOLASER CANNONS AND 60 HEAVY ION CANNON EMPLACEMENTS; 10 TRACTOR BEAM PROJECTORS; PARKING ON TOP OF SMALLER SHIPS (SORT OF AN "ACCIDENTAL WEAPON")

TOP SPEED: 975 KPH IN ATMOSPHERE (UNLESS THEY STOP AT A DRIVE-THRU WINDOW TO GET SOME IMPERIAL FAST FOOD)

STATS

- CONTROL
- HULL
- MANEUVER
- SPEED
- FIREPOWER
- MASSIVE GLOVE COMPARTMENT (FULL OF MANY SMALLER STAR DESTROYERS)

THE SHOWDOWNS

CHEWBACCA VS. JAWAS

WINNER: CHEWBACCA.

Although the Jawas are resourceful, picking a fight with a Wookiee is like flirting with disaster (and disaster's older sister, dismemberment). With a mighty sweep of his arm, Chewbacca sends all three of the Jawas backward, knocking them into one another like bowling pins. Tiny, grunting, hoodie-wearing bowling pins.

HOTH LUKE VS. TROPICAL DARTH MAUL

WINNER: HOTH LUKE.

Normally, Darth Maul is focused and alert, but he's still in "vacation mode," and therefore vulnerable (as well as jet-lagged). Hoth Luke sees this and disarms his foe, but that's pretty easy to do since the Sith Lord is in the middle of a nap.

QUI-GON JINN VS. COUNT DOOKU

WINNER: COUNT DOOKU.

By focusing on his anger, Dooku calls upon a barrage of Force lightning, which zaps Qui-Gon, making the Jedi look like a kindhearted charcoal briquette.

OBI-WAN KENOBI VS. THE INQUISITOR

WINNER: OBI-WAN KENOBI.

The Inquisitor might be the showier of the two, but his twirls and spins prevent him from making contact with Obi-Wan. They do not, however, prevent Obi-Wan from disarming his foe, who quits his job as an Inquisitor and becomes a street mime (which he totally resembles, with the white face and the red markings and the dramatic gestures and such).

LEIA VS. GREEDO

WINNER: LEIA.

Greedo is relentless in his pursuit, but Leia actually knows what she's doing. So with a few well-timed moves, the Princess gains the upper hand . . . and she writes the word LOSER on Greedo's forehead. (Okay, she doesn't do THAT, but she DOES win.)

HAN SOLO VS. JANGO FETT

WINNER: HAN SOLO.

Fett hits Solo with everything, even the kitchen sink (yup, Jango totally carries one of those around with him). But in the end, Han Solo uses his blaster to burn a hole in the bounty hunter's jetpack, rendering it useless and allowing Solo to stun Fett. Not with his blaster, but with surprisingly scandalous gossip.

ANAKIN SKYWALKER VS. JEK-14

WINNER: ANAKIN SKYWALKER.

JEK-14 thinks that Anakin is just another Jedi, reluctant to tap into his anger. Little does he know that Anakin had an anger sandwich just moments ago . . . and it was DELICIOUS! JEK-14 discovers that Anakin's rage equals his own, leaving the clone to observe, "And I thought I had issues . . ."

EZRA BRIDGER VS. BOBA FETT

WINNER: BOBA FETT.

Ezra may have been trained by a Jedi, but Boba Fett has been trained by the sneakiest sneaks in the sneaky-verse. Ultimately, it's Boba who's left standing, and Ezra who's left crying into his apple juice.

WICKET W. WARRICK VS. MAX REBO

WINNER: WICKET W. WARRICK.

Wicket knows he's outmatched, so he simply reads the musician bad reviews of his latest album. When he can stand no more, Max Rebo surrenders to the cuddly teddy bear—er, Ewok.

LANDO CALRISSIAN VS. EMPEROR PALPATINE

WINNER: EMPEROR PALPATINE.

Calrissian oozes charm, but that has no effect on Palpatine, who just plain oozes. And festers. Like a maggot wearing human clothes. Rather than unleashing a bolt of Force lightning, the Emperor simply mutters, "Your clothes are out of style." This wounds Lando more than any physical attack, and he collapses.

PADMÉ NABERRIE VS. STORMTROOPER
WINNER: PADMÉ.

Both opponents appear to be equally matched in terms of weapons. But Padmé is the better shot of the two, and way, way smarter. She simply waits for her adversary's blaster to overheat, then takes him out.

KI-ADI-MUNDI VS. ASAJJ VENTRESS
WINNER: KI-ADI-MUNDI.

Ventress is powerful, and at first it appears that she has the edge. But the more she caves in to her emotions, the easier it is for her Cerean adversary to calmly repel her onslaught. And while he does so, Mundi asks the unnerving question, "What's the matter? Can't take your eyes off my giant head?" The more she tries not to think about it, the more she does. Soon, Mundi stands triumphant . . . and so does his enormous noggin.

R2-D2 & C-3PO VS. JABBA THE HUTT
WINNER: JABBA THE HUTT.

The two droids are good-hearted, but mighty Jabba eats good-hearted droids for breakfast . . . literally. Eventually, Jabba tires of this farce and slams R2-D2 and C-3PO into an electrical socket, frying their circuits. Then he wonders whether they'd look better as statues in his garden or as decorations on his barge. Decisions, decisions . . .

POE DAMERON VS. SAVAGE OPRESS
WINNER: POE DAMERON.

Poe exits his craft in order to engage his enemy face-to-face, and Opress thinks he has Poe where he wants him. He keeps his eyes on Poe's blaster, but he doesn't keep his eyes on Poe's other hand, which has a pie in it. WHAP! Opress gets a pie in the face, which gives Poe time to restrain him. But at least he gets a delicious dessert out of the experience!

BB-8 VS. TUSKEN RAIDER
WINNER: TUSKEN RAIDER.

The nimble droid almost outmaneuvers the crazed assault of the Tusken Raider, but in the end, the desert warrior has BB-8 where he wants it . . . dressed in a teddy bear costume and occupying a special place among the other cute stuffed animals on the Tusken Raider's bed!

REY VS. RANCOR
WINNER: REY.

The rancor is formidable, but Rey escapes his grasp time and again, moving with the grace of a dancer. A dancer that tap-dances on the rancor's head until the mighty creature passes out. From that day forward, the rancor will run screaming whenever he sees a pair of tap shoes!

YODA VS. DARTH VADER
WINNER: YODA.

Yoda may be a little guy, but he has many tricks up those very short sleeves. Vader relies on fear and intimidation, but Yoda is unafraid . . . and tiny. Scurrying up the Dark Lord's pant leg, the Jedi Master rewires the circuitry in Vader's life-support system, causing an immediate system-wide shutdown. Soon, Vader topples over, unable to move. Who da man? YODA man!

JEDI LUKE VS. GENERAL GRIEVOUS
WINNER: JEDI LUKE.

Grievous tries to frighten the young Jedi with his four colorful whirling lightsabers, which make him look like an evil cyborg Christmas tree. But Skywalker has a calm that cannot be broken. Using the Force, Luke disarms the droid general, and soon the Jedi holds ALL of Grievous's lightsabers. He holds two in his hands, one between his teeth, and another between his toes, but he HOLDS them, dagnabbit!

ADMIRAL ACKBAR VS. BIB FORTUNA
WINNER: ADMIRAL ACKBAR.

Bib Fortuna has scary forehead-knobs and jagged fangs, but Ackbar has smarts. Thinking quickly, the admiral grabs Fortuna's brain-tails and ties them around the Twi'lek's hands like fleshy handcuffs. There, Ackbar thinks to himself. THAT's using your brain (-tails).

FINN VS. DARTH MALGUS
WINNER: DARTH MALGUS.

Finn fights valiantly, but the armored Sith Lord unleashes a tsunami of Force lightning on the ex-stormtrooper, forcing Finn to surrender . . . and to think to himself, "Well, this still beats being a stormtrooper!"

PONG KRELL VS. CAPTAIN PHASMA
WINNER: CAPTAIN PHASMA.

Pong Krell may be a Jedi, and one who can wield multiple lightsabers simultaneously, but he has nothing on the crazy-disciplined tactical know-how of Captain Phasma, who uses her First Order handcuffs (two sets of them, of course) to subdue her foe . . . after which she does a little victory dance.

MACE WINDU VS. KYLO REN
WINNER: KYLO REN.

Mace Windu wears his opponent down, but then the Jedi Master accidentally trips on Kylo Ren's super-long cape, giving Ren the advantage. Mace doesn't know which is worse; the defeat, or the fact that the other Jedis will never let him hear the end of it.

PLO KOON VS. TASU LEECH
WINNER: PLO KOON.

Plo disables many of Tasu's weapons, leaving him vulnerable. So vulnerable, in fact, that Tasu starts to cry. Plo gives him tissues, because he may have won the day, but he's not a jerk.

ANAKIN'S JEDI STARFIGHTER VS. KYLO REN'S COMMAND SHUTTLE
WINNER: ANAKIN'S JEDI STARFIGHTER.

It's no contest; Anakin's starfighter runs circles around the Command Shuttle. Literally. Until the Command Shuttle's crew gets nauseous and sick. Hey, no one said face-offs were pretty.

WOOKIEE GUNSHIP VS. FIRST ORDER SPECIAL FORCES TIE FIGHTER
WINNER: FIRST ORDER SPECIAL FORCES TIE FIGHTER.

Although the gunship has some impressive moves, the Special Forces TIE fighter destroys the modest craft, causing the Wookiees inside to run screaming "GNAARRRR!" (Which translates to, "Dude, those Special Forces guys are SUCH a buzzkill!")

POE'S X-WING VS. SITH INFILTRATOR
WINNER: POE'S X-WING.

The Sith Infiltrator exhausts itself firing on Poe's X-wing, which returns fire, and soon the Infiltrator is banged up so bad that Darth Maul can't even unload it on a "Used Infiltrator" dealership.

REY'S SPEEDER VS. AT-AT
WINNER: REY'S SPEEDER.

The AT-AT is heavily armored, but Rey repeatedly rams her speeder into its legs, causing them to give way until the metal monstrosity falls over. All Rey can think is, "Now, THIS AT-AT would make a MUCH nicer place to live in!"

MILLENNIUM FALCON VS. TIE ADVANCED PROTOTYPE
WINNER: *MILLENNIUM FALCON*.

The TIE Advanced Prototype boasts cutting-edge tech, and successfully outmaneuvers the *Millennium Falcon* at every turn. Until the *Falcon* decides to park herself DIRECTLY ON TOP of the TIE Advanced, SQUISHING it like an evil little bug.

NABOO STARFIGHTER VS. IMPERIAL STAR DESTROYER
WINNER: IMPERIAL STAR DESTROYER.

The Star Destroyer's captain feels sorry for the plucky Naboo fighter, so the Imperial warship only sends a dozen or so shuttles to demolish the tiny yellow vessel. But as a show of respect for the little royal engine that couldn't, the Star Destroyer uses the Naboo starfighter as a hood ornament.